On a Hot, Hot Day

Enjoy reading!

love ♡ Nicki Weiss 1993

Nicki Weiss

On a Hot, Hot Day

A TRUMPET CLUB SPECIAL EDITION

Published by The Trumpet Club
666 Fifth Avenue, New York, New York 10103

Text and illustrations copyright © 1992 by Monica J. Weiss

ISBN 0-440-83092-3

This edition published by arrangement with The Putnam
& Grosset Group

Designed by Nanette Stevenson and Colleen Flis.
The text is set in Bryn Mawr Book.

Printed in the United States of America
April 1993

10 9 8 7 6 5 4 3 2 1
UPR

For Zvia, Amikam, Rachel, Matan, Hadas, and Itai

On a hot, hot day
On a hot summer day

Mama says, "Think cool. Think cool."

So they spray their arms and toes and knees,
And pretend they're wading in the icy seas.

In the summer
The hot, hot summer
Mama swings her Angel.

On a rainy day
On a rainy fall day

Mama says, "Sip slow. Sip Slow."

So they blow on their cocoa in the luncheonette,
As the passersby outside get wet.

In the fall
The rainy fall
Mama twirls her Angel.

On a cold, cold day
On a cold winter day

Mama says, "Bundle up. Bundle up."

Then they shake the snow from their coats and hair,
And read all day in the big green chair.

In the winter
The cold, cold winter
Mama rocks her Angel.

On a breezy day
On a breezy spring day

Mama says, "Breathe deep. Breathe deep."

So they smell the mint and chive and dill
That Mama planted on the windowsill.

In the spring
The breezy spring
Mama hugs her Angel.

On any old day
At the end of the day

Mama says, "Good night. Sleep tight."

And she gives a hug, a twirl, a swing,
And tucks him in and starts to sing: